# Zhū 珠 Pearl

# Zhū 珠 Pearl

## DAUGHTERS OF WAR

Jasemin Sibo Sībǎo 思宝

PARTRIDGE

A Penguin Random House Company

**To order additional copies of this book, contact**
Toll Free 800 101 2657 (Singapore)
Toll Free 1 800 81 7340 (Malaysia)
orders.singapore@partridgepublishing.com

www.partridgepublishing.com/singapore

# Contents

# Daughters of War

*According to early Chinese civilization,*
*pearls symbolizes wisdom acquired through*
*years of experience and struggles.*

*These luminescent spheres are believed to attract*
*wealth and luck as well as offer protection. Known*
*for their calming effect, pearls can balance one's*
*karma, strengthen relationships, and keep children*
*safe. The pearl is also said to symbolize the purity,*
*generosity, integrity, and loyalty of its wearer.*

*Black pearls, were believed to have formed within*
*a dragon's head. Once full-grown, the pearls were*
*carried between the dragon's teeth. According to*
*this myth, one had to slay the dragon to gather*
*these highly sought after black pearls.*

*Wizened Japanese tells a tale of pearls being created from sorrowful tears of mythical creatures. Mermaids, nymphs and angels' tear drops birthed these glistening wonder carrying their tales of often forsaken love.*

*One Persian legend tells that pearls were created when a rainbow met the earth after a storm. Imperfections in a pearl's appearance were thought to be the result of thunder and lightning.*

*The ancient Egyptians prized pearls so much that they were buried with them. Cleopatra reportedly dissolved a pearl from one of her earrings in a glass of either wine or vinegar, depending on the source, and drank it. She did this just to show Mark Anthony that she could devour the wealth of an entire nation in just one gulp.*

## Synopsis

This book tells the story of two Chinese ladies.

Jade 玉 yu, born into a rich family in Guangzhou 广州Guǎngzhōu, China with a tycoon father and a socialite mother. From the day she was born, Jade had been groomed to be married into a life of luxury and prestige. Marriage and garnering the role as a lady of leisure 太太 tai tai, have been ingrained into her that it was the ultimate nirvana-like path for a woman to have a comfortable life.

Only through attracting a wealthy man, one that saw her worthy of 'being taken care of' would she avoid a lowly life. It was only through the magnanimity of her husband would Jade be able to have a good life. Being married off as soon as she was accepted by the first wealthy man was her parents' aspirations for her, and thus relinquishing their parental duties to provide for their daughter.

On the other side of the country not too far off from Guǎngzhōu, Teak 柚 you was born into a life of poverty. Teak's family lived in a remote village in Sichuan 四川Sìchuān. Her father was a farmer, and her mother was illiterate and partially blind. From the day she was born, Teak had been groomed to be a servant maid 工人 gōng rén.

Marriage and pursuing her dreams were never made privy to her, and she had been ingrained that her ultimate nirvana-like path would be to find a household that would take her in as a servant maid thus avoiding being a beggar. Earning money as soon as she was accepted by the first household was her parents' aspirations for her, and thus relinquishing their parental duties to provide for their daughter.

This book tells the tale of how these two women; an aristocrat and servant maid came to meet in the quiet town of Ipoh怡保 Yí bǎo. A hidden valley tucked in the midst of sprawling Peninsular Malaya. One cannot be called foolish to believe that perhaps it was the deities and goddesses from the heavenly realm that brought these two lives of polar opposites together. As their lives intertwine, neither of them could have imagined how they would forge an endearing bond.

One almost as strong as blood sisters in itself.

Neither of them could foresee that as they journeyed through their own separate lives, that tragedies, force majeure, infidelity and ruthless family in-fighting would bring them closer together through shared tears, joint grieving and many moments of simply not allowing the other sister to crumble and break into pieces.

Jade 玉 yu, a vision of fragility and elitism.

Teak 柚 you, an image of sturdiness and hardiness.

Both precious in their own right.

And such are us women, regardless of whether we are powerful head of states, celebrated global celebrities or a contented home maker, we embody bits of 'Jade' and 'Teak' weaved within the intricate fibres of our beings.

May this book remind you of the beauty which is innately in all of us.

God has bestowed us the gift of childbirth, motherly instincts and multi-tasking abilities, strengthened with a keen sense of women intuition. These soft powers are not to be trivialized and many have opined that it is even more powerful than the sophisticated supercomputers of our present days.

As I watched a mother caring for her new born baby, I cannot help but to be in awe at how she

could instinctively gauge her baby's needs from
just deciphering the baby's different manner
of crying and minute body language.

I cannot find an equivalent super processor that
could match this motherly instinct, even the one with
the most advanced artificial intelligence built in.

Perhaps the ultimate credit and honour should go to the
most powerful super being that exists within our midst.

One that created the heavens and earth, water, air
and fire. All the elements, animate and inanimate
objects that cover this wondrous blue planet of ours.

*God*

*Shàngdì*

上帝

This book has been written to honour one of God's most

beautiful creations. A creation that is so majestic, wise,

pure, where no two beings are ever created the same.

An ethereal being with a perpetual glow.

Each one a precious gem in her own right.


My dear friends, 朋友 péng yǒu, we

are these pearls personified.


*Zhu*

珠

*Pearl*

## Origin

This book is not about finding hidden pearls
in the depths of the ocean. It is also not about
examining and scrutinizing previous poet's
ode to this sacred underwater gem.

This book is a simple tale about Jade and
Teak, two Chinese ladies from vastly different
backgrounds, whom, through destiny see their
lives crossing paths and cementing an enduring
sisterly bond which spans a few decades.

Their stories also portray a current universal
phenomenon, where we observe mass exodus

of women treading unfamiliar territories in search of a better life. Be it in search of a new career opportunity, forgetting a past life, pursuing a new love interest, providing a better quality of life for her children, or even fleeing from oppression, wars and injustice….the list can truly be endless.

One thing for sure, it takes courage and unwavering inner strength to uproot oneself and charter new grounds. In all humility, I have been a diaspora, a permanent resident (not citizen), and an expatriate for about a decade of my life in 3 different countries.

The 1st year of arriving in your adopted country is often times the most trying. One would be juggling between acclimatizing to a new culture, building up a new social circle, and battling withdrawal symptoms of all kinds from the most menial to the more significant ones.

In the Asian context, unity and family cohesiveness defines a person. So when one leaves her country,

she is not only leaving her family behind but she
is also metaphorically speaking 'cutting off the
umbilical cord.' Stemming from this begs the question
of how then can one still perform acts of filial
piety and fulfill her responsibilities to her parents,
siblings and her other dependents from afar?

Feelings of guilt or even internal conflict may be
experienced by some during this point of transition.
However, in my humble opinion, time always heals and
time always tells. Time, has been said, is an instrument
used by God to smoothen the ruffled feathers and
tame the wild seas of emotions one may feel.

*Fate brings people together no matter*
*how far apart they may be*
有缘千里来相会
*yǒu yuán qiān lǐ lái xiāng huì*

## In Honor

This book is to honor women who have left their 'motherland', whether by circumstances or by choice. It pays homage to their courage and sacrifices made in leaving behind their old identities in replace of a new, perhaps infinitely awkward new identities in their adopted country.

Have you ever wondered why most country leaders have referred to their country of abode as 'her', and not 'he'? Motherland, Mother tongue and Mother Nature.

Without implying anything unbecoming, perhaps one can safely say that the term mother, she and her as a noun bears the resemblance of a woman, if a specific gender were to be accorded to it. And in the traditional context, what makes up of a woman? What are her traits? Gentleness, humility, loving, nurturing, forgiving and perhaps most important of all, putting everyone else's needs above her own.

*This book is for all women out there who have made sacrifices in the past, in the present and in the coming future….*

*To these brave women, you are indeed rare and precious pearls living within our midst.*

## Small Child

*小娃娃 xiǎo wá wa*

It was in the year 1927, 27th day of January that
Jade was born into a privileged home, with a servant
maid tending to her every whim and fancies from the
moment she opened her tiny almond shaped eyes.

Adorned in only the finest of silk clothing, with custom
made shoes covered in hand sewn embroidery,
one cannot blame her for thinking other girls lived a
similar lavish lifestyle like hers. Under the watchful
eye of her mother and her minder, Jade seldom
ventured out of the compounds of her home.

Daily routine involved various tutors teaching her the art of calligraphy, reciting Chinese poems, art of pruning bonsai trees, the practice of Chinese tea pouring and appreciation, mastering the 二胡 èr hú (a Chinese 2 string fiddle) and cooking Chinese delicacies for her parents and elders to savor.

Jade's parents made a deliberate attempt to preserve their daughter's delicateness by barring her from engaging in any activity that might ruin her complexion, skin or delicate fingers. Their daughter's prized asset was meant to be her looks, charm, poise and artistic talents.

Such was Jade's life up until she was 7, when sudden upheaval and political unrest would see her packing her bags in haste one night, with her father shouting at the family to hurry up else risk missing the boat ride that very night.

Jade's life was about to change, and as she clutched tightly onto her beloved porcelain doll that have become her inseparable companion, that would be the last time she would ever set foot in her motherland.

It was in the year 1927, 16th day of November that Teak, an unplanned child, was born. As her parents barely could feed themselves, having a child seemed like a far fetched luxury to the poor couple. But fate has it that Teak was to be brought into this world, into an impoverished lifestyle, where most times she would be left alone on her tattered thin mattress as both father and mother toiled in the fields.

Adorned in clothing made of cheap coarse linen, and running around bare feet most times, one cannot blame her for thinking other girls lived in a similar meager lifestyle like hers. Without the watchful eye of her mother, Teak seldom stayed indoors and could be found running across the corn fields and catching butterflies.

Daily routine involved being a helper to her mother as she toiled the fields, gathering corn and shucking these golden beads afterwards. Teak's knowledge of the world came from stories as told by her parents and friends, coupled with her own unbridled imagination of this seemingly boundless world.

Teak's parents made a deliberate attempt to toughen their daughter's sturdiness by teaching her the virtues of hard labor and learning new skills through mimicking others. Their daughter's prized asset was meant to be her brawn, adaptability, resilience and an iron-clad will to survive.

Such was Teak's life up until she was 7, when sudden upheaval and political unrest would see her packing her little possessions in haste one morning, as her father cried as he bade farewell to his precious land which has soaked in years of his sweat, tears and at times blood.

Teak's life was about to change, and as she touched
the edge of her cotton handkerchief that have become
her inseparable companion, that would be the last
time she would ever set foot in her motherland.

## Fleeing Motherland

*我的祖国 wǒ de zǔ guó*

It has been recorded in history that the Chinese Civil War erupted in August 1927 between the Kuomintang (KMT) which was Republic of China government led and the Communist Party of China (CPC).

Cessation of major active battles in 1950 saw the end of this war and spawned two factions being the Republic of China (ROC) in Taiwan and the People's Republic of China (PRC) in mainland China. Both have claimed to be the rightful legitimate government of China. Ideological differences relating to Communism vs. Nationalism was cited as the catalyst to this battle within Motherland China.

The civil war continued until late 1937, when the two parties joined forces forming the Second United Front to counter a Japanese invasion. China's full-scale civil war resumed in 1946 just a year after the end of hostilities with Japan.

The year 1950 marked the end of major military hostilities, with Republic of China's jurisdiction being restricted to Taiwan, Quemoy, Matsu, Penghu, and several outlying islands and the newly founded People's Republic of China controlling mainland China (including Hainan).

It was during this time of uncertainty, period of unforeseen unrest, in the year 1934, which saw Jade and Teak leaving their beloved motherland behind. They were to head down south, towards at that time this untamed terrain called Peninsular Malaya.

Their parents told them tales about this foreign place, thick with rainforests where tigers, monkeys and mouse deers roam free. The girls listened intently, both on separate occasions, both in different settings, but both ultimately heading towards the same final destination. This strange and bewildering place where they will call home.

Their fathers were just two out of the hundreds and thousands of Chinese immigrants flooding into Ipoh, a quiet town located on the North West of Peninsular Malaya during that period.

Ipoh, the city that tin built flourished from a tin mine boom back in the 1920s which lasted until late 1970s when prices of tin crashed and British controlled tin mining companies shut down.

This city, surrounded by scenic mountains is a valley, and have been on numerous occasions been unofficially termed as the Guilin 桂林 Guìlín of Malaya.

Now at this juncture, I feel compelled to share with

you one aspect which makes Ipoh quite unique. It

has been proclaimed by many, from near and far,

by explorers from the West to the traders from the

East that the fairest maiden in the whole of Malaya

hails from this small unassuming town of Ipoh.

Ipoh women harbor a secret, which has been quietly

passed down from one generation to the next.

Legend has it that the secret to Ipoh ladies' famed

beauty is in the water they consume and bathe in.

For you see, this picturesque valley is 'protected'

by many forbidding looking mountains and

limestone cliffs. And, it is believed the water that

flows from these God made giants carry natural

anti-ageing and skin rejuvenation particles.

A well-guarded elixir of youth, some say.

Is it an old wives tale? A myth? Urban legend perhaps?

I cannot say.

Perhaps one will have to experience it for
oneself and be one's own judge.

So as Jade and Teak bade their teary farewell
to their beloved Motherland which was now
torn by conflict and war, they clung on to
this hope of having a better life in Ipoh.

How is life going to turn out in this seemingly
mythical place where wildebeest abound, precious
tin are embedded deep within the soils of the earth
and a panacea for perpetual beauty awaits?

*All things are difficult before they are easy*

万事开头难

*wàn shì kāi tóu nán*

## People Mountain, People Sea

人山人海 *Ren shan ren hai*

Jade and Teak's new life in Ipoh town was vastly different from their sparsely populated villages. The tin mine rush saw tons of new immigrants flooding into Ipoh almost in droves of hundreds every other month. This once sleepy ghost town suddenly sprang to life, as the allure of seemingly instant wealth and overnight millionaires attracted opportunists and capitalists alike.

Jade's family brought over a sizeable amount of cash and gold nuggets and quickly sat up their new home near the town fringe. Jade's father, through a distant cousin who was now quite a formidable senior

officer in one of the tin mine corporations found him

a position as a junior staff within his company.

Through leveraging off his connections and currying

favor with his higher ranked cousin thus putting the

art of guanxi关系 guānxi in action, he quickly rose

up the ranks and soon found himself cementing his

future alongside his cousin in the same department.

Back in that era, British senior management relied

heavily on recommendations from their trusted

local counterparts. These colonist understood the

importance of forging close ties with 'nodes' of the

local cliques in ensuring a team of competent and

trustworthy workers would be hired on board.

Jade's father also heard tales from his cousin of

how 'ruthless' these British colonial masters can be,

as they would fire incompetent workers which were

deemed unscrupulous, practiced corruption or abused company's assets and intellectual properties.

To Jade's father, all these seemed very harsh, as in his mind the workers were just trying to make a living and provide food for their family and a roof over their heads.

"People will make mistakes and what is the real harm in telling one or two white lies. The bosses are well off enough already, surely missing a few mining tools will not hurt their pockets."

He kept these thoughts to himself and never shared with anyone. He would soon learn the numerous business and cultural differences in this foreign land, working in a corporation governed by foreigners unlike his own kind.

Teak's family arrived in Ipoh with barely any money or anything remotely valuable. Their prized possessions were the sacks on their backs with just a few pieces of linen clothes bolstered by their tenacity for hard work.

Teak's father, not knowing anyone in Ipoh saw

him quickly making friends around his local shack

his family now called home. His neighbors were

mostly low level laborers at the tin mines and soon

one kind Samaritan offered to introduce him to his

supervisor. As this supervisor also made his way

up the hard way, relying on no connections at all,

he empathized with this eager looking man, albeit a

bit weary looking and told him to come to the mines

the next day. Through sheer tenacity, hard work and

resilience, Teak's father was able to keep his role

and even became the head of the other laborers.

Teak's father was often reminded by his peers to

be courteous and respectful towards his British

bosses. These Anglo-Saxons were observed to

be strict, even intimidating if the situation arises.

There was one incident when members of a highly

feared triad attempted to extort them for 'protection

money.' Not only did these Colonists refused to kowtow

叩头 kòutóu to them, they threatened to call up the local authorities should they not leave their site immediately.

So, imagine Teak's father's delight when one day when he was toiling under the scorching hot sun; someone tapped on his shoulder and offered him a drink. When he turned around, he saw that it was one of the senior British managers holding out a cup of iced water with a grin on his face.

"Should I take the cup?

Will I appear disrespectful if I drink it in front of him or will I offend him if I refuse his offer?

Is this a test?"

"Not to worry my lad, I have seen how hard you have worked. I appreciate good and honest workers. Go on, take the cup."

As Teak's father gulped down the cool water and felt his scorched throat moistening, he suddenly felt an unusual kinship between him and this regal looking foreigner with kind eyes and a warm smile.

These two comrades, who had left their Motherland in the same year in 1934, and arrived in this strange town called Ipoh, soon found themselves immersing in a totally new vocation, working under British Colonial heads, and ultimately trying to forge a new future for themselves and their families.

*It is easy to find a thousand soldiers,*
*but hard to find a good general*
千军易得, 一将难求
*qiān jūn yì dé, yī jiang nán qiú*

Monday, 15 December 1941.

Ipoh was invaded by the Japanese.


The Japanese Occupation saw them

conquering several other Malaya states

including Penang, Jitra and Alor Setar.


It was during this period in the history of Ipoh that the

city established itself as an administrative centre, as

well as a commercial mining hub, and the Japanese

made Ipoh the state capital of Perak instead of Taiping.

In March 1942, the Japanese Civil Administration or

Perak Shu Seicho had been set up at the St. Michael's

Institution opposite the Ipoh Padang (field in Malay).


Jade and Teak's family fled and hid in the jungles

off Ipoh. They survived by eating shoots, wild spuds

and jungle ferns. They would hear the occasional

bombs going off and sirens blaring loudly in the

sky. Horror stories were passed along of rape and

torture conducted by the Imperial army. The girls

prayed in their hearts that all this atrocity would cease soon. Their family did not risk their lives fleeing their Motherland to be faced with another war.

The Japanese Occupation was brief.

On 15 August 1945 the Japanese announced the end of World War II. After the liberation of Malaya by British forces, Ipoh remained the capital of Perak, till this day.

*As a man sows, so he shall reap*
*Good for good, and evil for evil*
*种瓜得瓜, 种豆得豆*
*zhòng guā dé guā, zhòng dòu dé dòu*

## Born to be a Good Wife and Loving Mother

*賢妻良母 xián qī liáng mǔ*

Now, at this juncture, you may be wondering on the whereabouts of the two girls.

During the Chinese feudal times, a man would look for a wife that could take care of his offspring and manage the household while he toiled outside to earn a living. Men were providers, and women were taught to be submissive loyal wives.

An old adage goes, 'a wife should be blind to her husband's misdeeds' was an unspoken rule in a Chinese household. As long as the husband provided food on the table and a roof over her head, everything else is forgivable.

In the times of old China, sons were highly favored as they were seen as carriers of the family name hence sustaining the lineage. A son was also seen as the family's 'work horse', a provider to his family, care giver to his dependents and that of his wife's as well. The heaviest burden undoubtedly rests on the shoulders of the eldest son, for he inherits all the responsibilities and duties of that of his father.

As a countenance to this mountainous responsibility, the eldest son will be accorded certain privileges including total obedience from his younger siblings and veto rights pertaining to family matters. One can safely say, this privilege can be either a blessing or a curse depending on the capabilities & desires of the eldest son.

Now Jade and Teak have just turned 16 years old.

It was the year of the Water Goat in 1943.

In their mother's eyes, from the day they gave birth

to their daughters, they would never be theirs. It

was almost a rule that daughters were to be married

off, and carry her husband's family name.

An unmarried woman would be called a spinster,

left on the shelf, rejected goods even. And

once a daughter is married off, her parents'

role have been relinquished and she would be

her husband's 'property', under his charge.

So according to their mothers and female relatives, 16

was a ripe age to be married off to a kind benefactor.

In those days, husbands were rarely called husbands.

Terms of endearment rarely existed between

married couples. A husband demanded utmost

reverence and loyalty from his wife, and the wife

expected their husbands to provide food and
shelter for her and her family. Showing physical
affections such as a hug or a peck on the cheek
and uttering sweet nothings were seen as
impractical or even disrespectful to the husband.

Wives in those days would use the term chieftain,
master, lord, benevolent one, and again emphasizing
reverence to the head of the family. Marriage of
equality and spouses being seen as equals were non-
existent and not practiced. A woman who meets her
husband's demands, never challenges his authority, and
satisfying his physical needs is seen as a good wife.

Not forgetting the ability to bear healthy children,
especially a 1st son as it is seen as bringing good
luck and prosperity to her husband and the family.

Jade had her fate sealed the moment her father became
one of the senior officers in the tin mining company.
As according to Chinese custom, marriage of equal

status was of utmost importance. A potential suitor coming from sound financial standing, bearing a good family name and comparable social status was the key factor in determining compatibility. Not age, educational background, looks or even common interests.

For you see, Jade was not looking for a soul mate. She was looking for a benefactor and a provider who would take care of her for the rest of her life. She had no intention to work and preferred to devote most of her time in bringing up her children and taking care of the household and her husband's needs.

Jade had undergone years of intensive grooming into an artisan and wife worthy of a noble partner. She had finesse in all the traditional Chinese arts including beauty, couture, culinary, poetry, traditional music instruments and calligraphy just to name a few.

Young girls at that impressionable age have often been reminded of this old adage; "If you

marry a chicken, you become a chicken, if
you marry a dog, you become a dog."

And Jade wanted to marry a dragon.

After several rounds of lunches orchestrated by a
matchmaker, Jade were to marry the son of her
father's colleague, a very eligible bachelor vied by
many young maidens then. He ran a successful
textile company and was from a reputable family.
More importantly, he was financially secure and
would be able to take care of her material needs.

Conversely, he also saw her as a trophy wife which
would certainly be the talk of the town and further
elevate his standing in the business world.

Jade would marry into nobility.

Teak by then was working for a household as one of
the servant maids and nanny. Due to her honesty,

hard work and affability the family treated her as

one of their own and she was adored by them.

Household rules often saw the maids eating at the

back of the kitchen, as sharing meals with those she

served was almost a career assassination move.

But her second family saw her as their own, and never

once was she made to feel isolated or degraded.

Teak never thought of marriage as she was a

free spirit at heart and relied on herself to provide

for her material needs. By then her parents had

passed away and she was left to fend for herself.

This spunky girl was very street smart and taught

herself many skills from crocheting, cooking,

learning local languages to even opening a

small bank account with a local bank.

All this was accomplished by a village girl who was

illiterate with no formal education. All she had was

the ferociousness to survive like a tiger. She did
not see her shortcomings or humble background
as a hindrance; she believed in all her heart
that she was the champion of her own fate.

Talk about sheer will power of the human spirit.

From years of diligent saving and investing, she
managed to buy herself a small house in a middle
class suburb. As fate has it, she met and fell in love
with a simpleton who had just migrated to Ipoh from
a fishing village. Love blossomed between them and
soon enough saw them hopping on his motorcycle
going on fishing expeditions and swimming in the
cool natural ponds and waterfalls. They would then
lie on the grass and talk for hours about nothing,
while looking at the full moon and counting stars.

Teak did not care about his background, whether
he had money or would he be able to provide for
her needs. She wanted to marry her soul mate.

Teak would marry into love.


*It is as impossible to find a perfect man,*

*as it is to find 100 percent pure gold*

人无完人，金无足赤

*rén wú wán rén, jīn wú zú chì*

## Enter the Red Door 洪 門 hongmen

### *The Child Bride without Bound Feet 裹脚 guǒ jiǎo*

Entering the Red Door 洪 門 hongmen. This would
be most young girls' childhood dream back in that
era. Entering the Red Door means to marry into
a rich family of status and power. As a woman's
identity back then hinges on her husband, once
you marry, the rest of your life is sealed.

Divorce back then was a taboo. So one may find many
unhappy marriages but the couple still live together for
fear of defying social norms or attracting ugly gossips.
Further, it was common practise for a wealthy man

to take on more than one wife or even mistresses, or concubines as what it was known back in those days.

Polygamy was rife and accepted. It was not something wives had a say against, it was seen as their fate. Some even say they were not performing their duties well enough hence pushing the husband to find another woman to make up for her shortcomings.

Jade's wedding day was a large celebration where the colour red could be seen covering the house, her attire to the red packets which were to be handed out to her younger relatives.

Her wedding preparations began eight months in advance, starting from the custom tailoring of her qibao 旗袍 qípáo or cheongsam 长衫 cháng shān, a one-piece Chinese traditional dress which has been worn since the Manchu ruled China in the 17th century.

The original qípáo was wide and baggy and featured a high neck and straight skirt. Not the most flattering on the female wearer. It covered all of a woman's body except for her head, hands, and toes. The qípáo was traditionally made of silk and featured intricate embroidery depending on how deep the payer's pockets were.

The qípáo worn today are modeled after ones made in Shanghai in the 1920s. The modern qípáo is a one-piece, formfitting, floor length dress that has a high slit on one or both sides. Trendier variations may have bell sleeves or be sleeveless and are made out of a variety of fabrics. Modern versions very much accentuate the female's sensual physique in an elegant manner.

A qípáo can take a few days to a few months to make, depending on the level of intricateness of the design. Jade's was hand sewn with traditional Chinese designs weaved with gold threads and small pearls.

Symbols of phoenix birds, dragons and peonies
can be seen symbolizing prosperity and luck.

In those days, cosmetics were mostly homemade and
Jade's female relatives helped to pound fine powder as
foundation to her face. Red paper would be used to tint
her lips red, and black charcoal used to outline her eyes.
Her hair was done up in an elaborate bun-like fashion,
with hair pins made out of the finest pearls and jade as
ornaments. She was a vision of elegance and prestige.

On the eve of her wedding day, she soaked her body
in a tub of warm water filled with flower petals. This
acted as perfume to her body, where hopefully the scent
would be pleasing to her husband on their wedding
night. Lest his wrath is roused by his new trophy wife
causing him to take on a few concubines in his disdain.

Teak's wedding day did not have the same
fanfare or elaborateness as that of Jade's. As

both she and her husband were poor, minimal money was spent on that happy occasion.

Nonetheless, their friends and families were overjoyed at the union of love and camaraderie. A simple luncheon and tea ceremony was performed at her new house, and the girls cooked up a storm with prosperity dishes such as steamed pomphret, drunken prawns in wine, jujube broiled chicken and poached kalian. Though the dishes were simple, the celebration and feelings of genuine joy was rich.

Teak had made her own simple qípáo a week before her wedding; it was of cheap silk with only peonies as embroideries. She tied up her hair in a simple bun and only had her lips tinted red. A minimalist and a frugal character, she did not believe in indulging even on her wedding day. What mattered to her was that her loved ones were there to celebrate this union and both husband and wife would journey their life together through thick and thin. Nothing else mattered. Teak was an image of simple happiness adorned in her own craft work.

Both the brides considered themselves to be very lucky to have escaped from the torturing practise of foot binding. Jade's mother was the last woman in her family to endure this ancient beauty ritual while Teak's mother, coming from a farmer's lineage, never practised this custom which was mostly accorded to the wealthy.

Foot binding 裹脚 guǒ jiǎo.

It is not clear at which point in history this practice began. This painful custom is believed to have birthed during the Tang and Song dynasties. Tenth century descriptions of "golden lotuses" in the royal courts are believed to be references to bound feet. According to one story, this torturous art of beauty was invented by a palace dancer who indulged the sadistic fancies of her royal master. According to another story, an emperor was seduced by a woman with small feet who performed on top of a lotus-shaped table and by royal decree ordered every woman to have her feet bound.

Writers in the 13th and 15th century have described these "exquisite feet" being "three inches long and no wider than a thumb." Some even mused: "Why must their feet be bound? To prevent the barbarous act of running around. If girls' feet were not bound, they go here and there with questionable acquaintances."

Guǒ jiǎo, performed on women throughout the 20th century was prevalent across Chinese society. Originating with the wealthier classes, it cascaded down through urban and then poorer rural communities over the years. Guǒ jiǎo survived for almost a millennium before gradually dying out.

Only women from the upper class society could afford to have it done as foot-bound women couldn't do physical work or move around much. Lower-class women needed working feet to do menial laborious work.

The process used to create bound feet was excruciating. Young girls from the tender age of 5 would have their feet broken and bound tightly with cotton strips. This forced their four smallest toes to fold under the soles thus creating a 3-inch golden lotus. Once the job was done, women would not walk but hobbled around. This was a true manifestation of an old Chinese saying being "wanting beauty over preserving one's life."

The process would last over the course of many years and a lifetime of labored movement, as well as a frequent need to rebind the feet.

There is a school of thought leaning to the notion that foot binding served as a strong multi-generational bond for women. Guǒ jiǎo was a tradition passed from mother to daughters, entangled with shoemaking, how to endure pain and how to attract men, albeit a less romantic notion once the actual process is made known. In many ways, it underpinned women's culture.

During the imperial era guǒ jiǎo was regarded as

the epitome of feminine beauty and an indication

of prestige. In the times of Communism the custom

was looked down as a primitive vestige of the feudal

era: its beauty defined by primitive thinking men.

I am pretty sure some of our more liberal Western

counterparts would be reeling by now. It is often a

point of deliberation on what would be deemed as

barbaric or a social norm. I guess it really would

depend on the culture, period of time we live in and

perhaps even a degree of social caste at play.

*No pain, no gain*

吃得苦中苦,方为人上人

*chī dé kǔ zhōng kǔ, fāng wéi rén shàng rén*

Both girls shared the same trepidation and excitement

as they were led into their bedrooms by their new

Chieftain for one, and a soul mate for the other.

The wedding night 洞房花烛夜 dòng fáng huā zhú yè was very important as the new brides would be gauged by their husbands as how well they could please them in the future.

Chinese husbands are traditionally very pragmatic beings, where they see their wives as having a 'duty' to satiate their sexual desires. This is not that far off from other cultures including for the Muslim men.

In the greater scheme of things, one can say this is to protect the sanctity of the marriage where the husband would not have a reason to commit infidelity or take on a concubine. Hence, one can imagine the pressure new brides back then felt as they consummate their marriage on the wedding night.

Jade and Teak recollected tales told by their grandmothers when they had to go through a 'virginity test' during dòng fáng.

On the bed would be placed a white handkerchief,

and the morning after this handkerchief was meant

to be displayed to the families as a testimony

to her virginity with drops of blood as proof.


In the event the evidence failed to emerge, the

husbands had the right to nullify their marriage

immediately. The once glowing brides would

then suffer banishment from the village and be

labelled as 'promiscuous' and 'immoral' and risk

being a spinster for the rest of their lives.

## Sisters

### 姐妹 *jiě mèi*

Now 10 years have passed for Jade and Teak. They are now 26 years of age having families of their own.

Jade has seven children and as her husband's business soared, so did his power, prominence and financial wealth. His thirst for younger fairer ladies grew and he took on two more younger wives which bestowed him with another four children.

However, Jade's position as the 1st wife coupled with the good fortune of bearing a son as the 1st child solidified her position within the three wives' ranking. In the days of Chinese feudal system, polygamy was widely practiced especially amongst the aristocrats and royalties.

Not only was it a testament of the men's' financial capability to provide for several wives and children, it was also regarded a good blessing on the men, for the sons he would have would carry on his family name after his eventual passing.

Consequently, it was commonplace to observe amongst the wives the inescapable politicking, manipulation, scheming and deploying ancient Chinese practices and chants to gain their Chieftain's affection and protect one's inheritance.

It was an open secret, in those days, that sons would get the lion share of their father's inheritance, with the daughters following suit. It was a doomed fate for most wives as it was widely practiced that they would not receive even a dime.

So, the few wise ones would save allowances given by their Chieftains or hope one of their filial sons would give them some of their inheritance once the fateful day comes.

An old Chinese saying again rings true;
*Like father like son*
有其父必有其子
*Yǒu qí fù bì yǒu qí zǐ*

For you see, Jade's father-in-law also had three wives so it was not surprising that Jade's husband followed suit. All Jade could do, was to ensure strong ties with her sons and played her cards right as the 1st wife.

In a family hierarchy of such, the 1st wife was seen as the elder sister 大姐 dà jiě by the two younger wives. They would be regarded as younger sisters 小妹 xiǎo mèi by Jade and by custom would have to consult Jade with every family matters including their children's welfare.

In times of harmony, the three ladies in the same household would live in peace with each having an almost equal amount of attention from the Chieftain. In times when inevitable squabbles are rife, one would observe conniving acts of scheming, manipulation or even slandering to weaken the more favored opponent. Schemes include concocting a 'lovesick' tea for the Chieftain to drink (believed to skew his affection towards the said wife), undergoing risky surgery to recreate a 'virgin's sensation' on the wife's nether region, to masterminding cruel smear campaigns on her opponents.

The reign of Empress Dowager Cixi 慈禧太后 Cí xǐ Tài hòu, possibly one of the most controversial and powerful rulers in Chinese history and has been widely documented in books, adapted into movies, television series and the like.

A common speculation behind her meteoric rise from a third grade concubine to an iconic status being 'The Concubine Who Launched Modern China' was by gaining favor with Empress Zhen, then principal wife to Emperor

Xian Feng. Further, hell hath no wrath like a woman's fury; such as the case when according to historians Cí xǐ orchestrated the death of a royal enemy for sabotaging her supposed love affair with a court eunuch.

Jade's life of supposed affluence and bliss was without its challenges. There is a price to pay for everything in life. Regardless, she was overall contented and tolerated the politicking and back biting so long as her privileged life did not suffer significant interruption.

Though she had been forbidden to see her own parents ever since she entered the red door, she saw it as a sacrifice she was willing to make in return for luxury.

In Jades eyes, *money is divine*
钱可通神 *qián kě tōng shén*

Teak, on the other hand, was enjoying a close knit family setting living close to her friends and extended family. She bore only one son, after many years of futile attempts and saw it as a gift from the Goddess of Mercy.

For many years, she had tried to conceive but failed. With a pious heart, she made diligent offerings to this deity she revered by burning joss sticks and giving alms to the temple's nuns and monks in the hope of sowing good karma.

One can say her plea was finally heard and a healthy baby boy was bestowed upon them.

Teak and her husband lived a simple life, with her still working in the same household as the servant maid and her husband working in a few construction sites as a laborer. At times, they barely had enough money to buy milk powder for their toddler son or were months in arrears on their mortgage payment. Still, life was good as they enjoyed each other's undivided companionship and reveled in life's simple pleasures.

Whilst Jade was rich in material wealth but poor in family bonding, Teak was rich in kinship and family bonding but poor in material wealth.

In Teak's eyes, *love is enough*
*有情飲水飽 yǒuqíng yǐnshuǐbǎo*

Who was happier, one may ask? I am not one to say.

For happiness is subjective, and is transient from one phase in life to the other.

Only the beholder can ascertain the true measure of happiness and contentment.

It was during this time, that Jade and Teak's life intertwined. One of Jade's maids had returned to her own village and wanted to start a farm. This prompted Jade to begin scouting for a new helper.

In those days, personal recommendations and referrals were the common modus operandi in looking for a servant maid. Upon asking a few neighborhood tai tais, Teak's name was mentioned several times.

"I must see this Teak lady personally. If so many tai tais have sung praises of her work, she must be of good character and a hardy worker."

One early morning, at the start of
the Winter Solstice festival

冬至 Dōngzhì, Jade went to the household where Teak worked. This marked their first encounter, on this day of 'the extreme of winter', and widely speculated to be the shortest day in the year. In certain parts of China, Dōngzhì overshadows the Chinese Lunar New Year 农历新年 nóng lì xīn nián celebration. This is largely due to the belief that the passing of Dōngzhì ushers in days with longer daylight hours, therefore enhancing positive qi 气 qì energy flowing in.

Thus this was how Jade and Teak met.

Two xiǎo wá wa who hailed from the same Motherland.

Born in the same year of the Rabbit, and conceived during the start of the Chinese Civil War.

Daughters of War whom, not by mere coincidence, would cross paths in their new found home in Ipoh.

Their maiden meeting was a brief albeit a concise one.

Jade was quick to make her requests known, and Teak was in no haste in giving her a reply on the spot. She needed some time to mull over things, as loyalty at that time was a highly ingrained virtue. Though Jade offered a higher salary, and she really needed the extra money as her son was to enter school soon, she was not sure whether leaving her current household would be one which she will regret in time to come.

Chinese astrologers have said that those born
in the year of the Rabbit are kind, affectionate,
obliging, and always pleasant. By the same token,
they may have a tendency, though, to get too
sentimental and overly cautious and conservative.

Teak could not reason out the strong
kinship she felt between them, as if they
had known each other for a long time.

"Perhaps in our past life, we were sisters. Or perhaps
due to past karma, we have met in this life for
reasons only the future will unfold," she thought.

Could it even be that these two 'Rabbits' had a chance
meeting when they first landed on the soils of Peninsular
Malaya, as their local middle man haphazardly
ushered them onto their respective vehicles?

*Time will tell.*

That evening, Teak and her family made and ate glutinous rice balls 湯圓 tangyuan. This Dōngzhi activity symbolizes family togetherness and the roundness of the tangyuan means unity.

Tangyuan are made of glutinous rice flour and sometimes brightly colored. Each family member receives at least one large tangyuan in addition to several small ones. The flour balls may be plain or stuffed with crushed peanuts or black sesame paste. They are often cooked in a ginger sweet soup with both the ball and the soup served in one bowl. Some families may serve it with a mildly alcoholic unfiltered rice wine containing whole grains of glutinous rice, and often also sweet osmanthus flowers.

As she lay on her bed, recollecting her earlier meeting with Jade, she prayed again to her beloved Goddess of Mercy and asked her to give her a sign if she wanted her to accept Jade's offer. That same night, Teak dreamt of a beautiful garden filled with chrysanthemums, jasmines, hibiscus and orchids. On the corner of the garden were pots of artistically trimmed bonsai trees. There were humming birds and dragonflies flying around this Garden of Eden, and it felt almost heavenly.

When Teak awoke the next morning, she saw her dream as a blessing from the deities to accept Jade's offer.

Peace of the heart is often used as an indicator to choosing a new path in life for those that follow Taoism or Confucianism.

It is not very dissimilar to the Christian practice of "following the peace of God."

It was the beginning of Dōngzhi that Jade and Teak met, and it was the end of Dōngzhi that these two strangers would fulfill their pre-determined destiny as sisters 姐妹 jiě mèi.

## Face 脸 liǎn

*Lose face, Thick Face, Face value*

Banquet 宴会 yànhuì

This would be the common affair in Jade's household, consisting now of the Chieftain, 3 wives, 11 children, 6 servant maids and a dozen other odd workers ranging from drivers, gardeners, cooks, tutors, midwives and handymen.

Teak was specially assigned to tend only to Jade's needs. Her duties include helping her now mistress to dress in many of her elaborate Chinese costumes to accompany the Chieftain during his official outings. The Chieftain has now been promoted to join the ranks of the highest local officers, being trusty aides to their British counterparts. The Chieftain was exposed to the game of croquet, cricket, horse riding and was also taught the card game gin rummy.

In reciprocal, the Chieftain imparted certain Chinese cultures to his British comrades such as saying yamsing 饮胜 yam seng when toasting whiskey, playing mahjong 麻将 má jiàng, and partaking in Prosperity Toss during Chinese Lunar New Year, also known in Cantonese as 捞起 lo hei in the form of a Teochew-style raw fish salad.

Jade was well favored by the wives of the British managers and the ladies formed a weekly group exchanging hobbies and the arts from the Western and Eastern continents.

The exquisite looking Jade, with her delicate features and fair skin, often was affectionately called "my pretty Chinese Doll" by her friends. She took a keen interest in earning how to crochet, recite her favorite Shakespeare poems and bake scones and muffins for high tea.

During her 30th birthday, she was presented with a white parasol decorated in fine lace and pink roses imprint. Jade was so ecstatic, she and Teak had a ball of a time walking around the garden with the parasol, pretending they were on the grounds of a British palace whilst sipping Earl Grey tea and singing "Ring around the Rosie."

During the many grand banquets which these wives would accompany their husbands, Jade taught her British sisters the art of using the chopsticks and appreciating Chinese tea. During one Chinese Lunar New Year, she presented each of the ladies a small Jade brooch. The Jade gemstone is believed to bless whatever it touches, and is the stone of calm in the midst of storm. The English Roses were beyond delighted upon receiving this precious gift from the Orient.

Teak and Jade's nightly heart to heart chats would often come to the same shared conclusion after a day's outing with their rosy cheeked British maidens;

*"A rose by any other name would smell just as sweet"*
玫瑰不管叫啥名,闻起来总是香的
*méi guī bù guǎn jiào shá míng, wén*
*qǐ lai zǒng shì xiāng de*

The same thoughts would play in the Chieftain's mind too as he lay rested in his chamber. He never envisioned his current reality, working alongside his British peers, being treated almost as an equal partner. One particular phrase from Deng Xiao Ping came into his mind;

*"It doesn't matter if a cat is black or white, so long as it catches mice"*
白猫黑猫,会捉老鼠就是好猫

*bái māo hēi māo, zhuā dào lǎo shǔ jiù shì hǎo māo*

How true.

Teak had celebrated 14 Dumpling festival 肉粽節 ròu zòng jié or also known as Dragon Boat festival 端午节 duān wǔ jié with her mistress and Chieftain. She could not believe that it has been 14 years she had served her mistress Jade.

Those years of making and eating zongzi and drinking realgar wine seemed so fresh in her mind still. She would turn melancholy as well as she reminisced about her childhood years in her Motherland. How she would race her father down to the edge of the river to watch the magnificent and brilliantly decorated dragon boats.

Jade regarded Teak beyond that of a servant maid. She was her loyal friend, comrade, confidante and sister. Teak would harbor many of her mistress's secrets and private anguishes as during the feudal times wives do not complain nor dare to show any disdain towards their benefactors.

This holds true even in instances when the husbands have committed 'abuses', verbal or physical. In that era of extreme Chinese conservatism, the epitome of a good wife is one where she can put on a smile even if her heart was breaking into pieces.

Such was the case when Jade discovered her Chieftain had been frequenting a notorious street tucked in the centre of bustling Ipoh Old town, Concubine Lane. As the name would suggest, this lane served as a dark haven for men.

Coolies from the tin mines used to be the frequent patrons to this lane, lined with brothels and opium dens during an age when such activities were conducted in a less-than-discreet manner. Now, Jade finds her Chieftain may have deposited a concubine there. These women of pleasure existed solely to give rich men worldly pleasures, and were cloistered away from sight, visited discreetly. Even though this 'woman of the night' will not hold any position in Jade's family, she cringed at the thought of her Chieftain in the arms of a 4th woman.

Jade went into a mild depression as her Chieftain spent less and less time with her. Within the current 3 wives setting, it was already a challenge vying for his attention. At times, months would go by before he would visit her in her chambers. Jade secretly envied Teak who would go back to her home every night into the arms of her devoted husband.

Teak would often try to cheer her sister up by cooking some of her favorite traditional dishes from their Motherland. One was Yam Abacus 算盘子 suan pan zi. Looking very similar to the modern Italian Gnocchi, it is made with fresh yam mixed with tapioca flour and turned into dough. After which, thumb size pieces of 'abacus' would be created using the cook's deft fingers, and indenting the middle as the final touch. Jade would then stir fry this with black fungus, dried shrimps, mushrooms, shredded carrots, celery and soy sauce. The preparation can take up to 2 hours to prepare these little flavorful gems.

During the cold rainy nights, Teak would concoct her own version of "Buddha Jump Over the Wall." Since its creation during the Qing Dynasty (1644 – 1912) the dish has been regarded as a Chinese delicacy privy to the rich and known for its rich taste, usage of various high-quality ingredients and special manner of cooking. The dish's name is an allusion to the dish's ability to entice the vegetarian monks from their temples to partake in the meat-based dish.

During her impoverished childhood days, Teak remembered her mother re-creating this dish by replacing the grossly expensive sharks fin, abalone, scallop and sea cucumber with shredded turnip, Monkey head mushroom, bamboo shoot and hard tofu boiled for hours in chicken broth.

Jasemin Sibo Sībǎo 思宝

*Tolerate 忍 ren*

This would be Jade's mantra ever since she entered the
Red Door. To tolerate her Chieftain's misdemeanors,
to tolerate her children's' unruly behavior, to tolerate
the 2 other wives and a concubine's existence.

All in the name of preserving family harmony.

To preserve her Chieftain's *face* 脸 liǎn,
at the cost of *losing her face*.

To put on a *thick face* in portraying the image
that everything is fine and well, at the cost
of her own private agony and shame.

To delude their neighbors and relatives when
they judge her based on *face value*.

Just to obtain their nod of approval for
being a 'good wife, loving mother.'

## Farewell. My Chieftain

再见 老板 *zài jiàn lǎo bǎn*

Quiet hushes and hastened footsteps could be
heard outside of the Chieftain's chambers.

The once mighty dragon of the house was now lying
on his deathbed, almost lifeless. He had been ill
for the past few months. At first, what appeared to
be symptoms of the common flu soon transformed
into skin rashes, high fever, uncontrollable
shivering, bloodied stool and vomiting of blood.

Western and Chinese medicine failed to treat him. From syringe injections, acupuncture to consuming herbal remedies boiled over the course of 24 hours. One male servant even offered his precious home brewed potion; small white mice soaked in rice wine kept for a year. Jade politely declined his sincere offer.

His 3 wives were stricken with fear. The concubine had ran away with a coolie, her secret lover of many years. Both had sacrificed their dignity and youth just to save enough money to start a new life, forgetting that their sordid past ever existed.

Jade fainted a few times when the doctors gave yet another bad news that her husband's health was worsening as the days went by. They were to prepare themselves for the inevitable.

Teak brought Jade to a renowned temple in the outskirts of Ipoh to seek divine help from her trusted Goddess of Mercy. The women burnt joss sticks, knelt on their knees and prayed for hours in front of the deity hoping their pleas will be heard.

Teak, the ever faithful friend and servant made a pact with her revered deity.

"Please heal my Master and in return I will forgo all forms of meat for a year, in your honor."

Jade never left her Chieftain's bedside and offered solace and words of comfort when he winged in pain. She made a solemn promise to herself that if her benefactor was healed, she would become a full fledge vegetarian as well.

It was exactly 12:30am on the 15th day of the 4th month in the year of the Fire Sheep 1967 that the Chieftain exhaled his last breath.

He was surrounded by his wives, children and his most loyal servants and helpers. Two of his

British managers, who by now have become
close friends, were at his bedside as well.

The Chieftain's death remained unknown. Some
rumored him to have contracted syphilis during one
of his nocturnal romps at Concubine Lane. There
was also speculation that he had contracted measles
or rubella which had no vaccination in that part of
the world at that period of time. In fact, even until
this day, reducing mortality rates due to measles
and rubella remain a key concern for 3rd world
and developing countries in South East Asia.

The Chieftain's funeral was a grandiose affair.
According to Chinese customs, no one was to don
in red for the loud color may provoke the wrath
of lingering spirits and is a form of disrespect
to the dearly departed and his next of kin.

The Buddhist centered funeral lasted for 49 days,
common for wealthy families, with the first 7 days

being the most important. Prayers were said every 7 days for 49 days. The age of the deceased, the cause of death, the fact that the deceased was single or married, the social status of the deceased are all factors that influence Chinese death rites.

Some superstitious family members vehemently believed the Chieftain's spirit would return to visit his loved ones on the 7th day of the funeral, escorted by the "Bull Head and Horse Face' soldiers from Hades.

With somber pragmatism, Jade and her son had in fact begun preparations for the funeral when the doctors jointly diagnosed the Chieftain as gravely ill. Jade's eldest son, being the eldest child in the entire clan would now be the head of the family. His duties among others would include relations with the family ancestors.

The Chieftain's children and daughters-in-law wore black, as black symbolized the strongest sadness. Grandchildren wore blue clothes. Sons-in-law then wore white or beige. The children and daughters-in-law also had a sackcloth hood placed on their head. Jade was clad in white, wailing and knelt beside her Chieftain's coffin. Relatives arriving later crawled on their knees towards the coffin to demonstrate their remorse.

It was also customary for blood relatives and daughters-in-law to wail and cry during mourning as a sign of respect and loyalty to the deceased. Wailing is particularly loud if the deceased has left a large fortune. As the Chieftain was wealthy, loud wailings echoed across the neighborhood.

Throughout this period of mourning, Teak never left Jade's side. She knew her mistress needed her. Many a times Jade collapsed during the 49 days ceremony and her able sister rushed to her side, helping her to sip water and fanning her flushed face.

She could not comprehend the depth of loss that her sister was now going through. The realization that someone you loved so dearly was now gone forever, into the netherworld. She hoped that when the same fate befalls on her, she could rely on Jade to share this painful grief and loss together. All Teak could do now, was to be a pillar of support for her suffering sister.

Ching Ming festival清明节Qingming Jie would mark the yearly event where Jade's eldest son would lead the entire clan to pay respects at his late father's tomb.

Translated as "Pure Brightness Festival," the name suggests a time for people to go outside and enjoy the greenery of springtime. However, it is mostly noted for its connection with Chinese ancestral veneration and the tending of family graves. Known also as "Tomb Sweeping Day," it is believed the departed Chieftain would be able to observe his family sweeping his tomb and savoring the food, tea, wine and joss paper accessories offered to his spirit.

Jasemin Sibo Sībǎo 思宝

As the Chieftain came from wealth, elaborate
joss paper accessories were burnt such as paper
cars, maids, house, money, mahjong set and
clothes for him to peruse in the netherworld.

Jade had devoted a good 24 years of her youth and
life to her benefactor. Though it was not a union of
passion and romance, she was grateful to him for
providing her and their children their material needs.
They never had to worry about money, or the lack of it.

As a sign of devotion, she made a vow to the same
Goddess of Mercy that Teak brought her to, to never
marry again. As a public declaration, she then tied her
hair in a bun and never had it changed ever since then.
Though she would not have defied Chinese customs
to remarry, it was her personal decision not to.

Some may rule out her act to be
harsh, even superstitious.

But I beg to differ.

What I see is an endearing love and promise
of one wife to her husband, an oath which
was still honored during life or afterlife.

*Flowers may bloom again, but a person*
*never has the chance to be young again*
*So don't waste your time*
花有重开日, 人无再少年
*huā yǒu chóng kāi rì, rén wú zài shào nián*

# The Awakening of Phoenix

*鳳起來 fèng qǐ lai*

The year of the galloping Horse ushered in 1978.

Chinese horoscope pointed to the 4th, 9th and 12th as lucky lunar months. Auspicious numbers were 2, 3, 7 and lucky flowers were calla lily and jasmine.

It has been 44 years since the two xiǎo wá wa left their beloved Motherland. A further 11 years had passed since the Chieftain's mysterious death. Jade and Teak are now 51 years old, wizened and very much adapted to the Malaya culture. Both speak fluent Bahasa, Cantonese, Mandarin, Queen's English, and sporadic Japanese from the brief Occupation coupled with a few Tamil words.

The Chieftain's family empire flourished under the eldest son's governance, and had spawned from a humble textile company into a regional conglomerate. The son, who was educated in London localized his overseas experience to fit into the Asian context. He succeeded in strategically fusing Western futurism and capitalist business models with the intricate Eastern cultures and socialist values.

At that period, Ipoh was at its peak of its economic boom. Chartered Bank of India, Australia and China opened offices here, and one could see the proliferation of accounting firms, real estate agents and brokers.

After the British regained control of Ipoh following the end of World War II, the city transformed into a centre of entertainment and the business

community learned to let the good times roll.

Cinema halls were erected by two of the largest

entertainment groups then, the Cathay Organisation

and Shaw Brothers Company. So too were amusement

parks, cabarets and after-hours clubs. Ipoh became

one of just four cities to be included among the

first destinations served by Malaysian Airlines.

Tin had made Ipoh an international city

that could be reached in a matter of

hours from anywhere in East Asia.

This tin city where the marriage of hard work and

trusted partnership between the local Chinese,

Malays, Indians and British counterparts built.

Things took a sudden turn when the tin industry

that had bolstered the local economy for so long

collapsed, prompting many workers to find employment

elsewhere in the newly independent Malaysia. Ipoh started to lose its luster and was slowly regressing into a ghost town, a pale shadow of its former self.

Jade and Teak, who were accorded major shareholdings in the family empire by the eldest son, refused to waiver amidst the chaos. It broke their hearts to see their beloved Ipoh being 'abandoned' by her people. Local talents and British executives began packing their bags heading home or seeking greener pastures.

It was a heart breaking period for Ipoh.

"Da jie, do you remember this proverb?"

*When people work with one mind,*
*they can even remove Mount Taishan*
人心齐, 泰山移
*rén xīn qí, tài shān yí*

Jade immediately read her younger sister's mind.

They knew what they had to do.

The sisters did not despair over what or whom they have lost. For times of calamity uncover true friends and serve as a test of one's mettle. They began seeking out other like-minded women all over Ipoh, regardless of ethnicity, religion, creed or social status.

"Ladies, join us for the greatest show on Earth!"

This was their battle cry.

With fervor, they garnered support from women in the nearby towns to rural villages, both young and old, astute to the illiterate.

For you see, just about 15 years ago, the year 1963, the sisters were mesmerized by a movie produced by Shaw Brothers (Hong Kong) entitled Love Parade.

The sisters were enamored by the loving

performance by then Malaysia's 1st celebrity

power couple the late Tan Sri P.Ramlee and

wife Datin Saloma, epitome of modern Malays

during the heyday of modern Malaysia.


In particular, was when the couple serenaded

a romantic version of Bengawan Solo.


Individually, they were a force to be reckoned with.


Together, they were an outstanding talented couple

who helped propel the Malaysian entertainment

industry into the international arena.


Love Parade was like a visual eclectic medley

of fashion, music, stage play, hairstyles from

cultures all over the world then. Artistically done,

it was not a simple feat amalgamating American

pop culture like Jackie-O infamous 'bob' hairdo,

Malay influenced figure accentuating Baju Kebaya

dresses, Chinese cheongsams topped with pearl necklaces and white-faced Japanese 'geishas' donned in fine silk Kimonos on the silver screen.

It was a 5-star cultural feast for the eyes.

Fast forward to 1969, the Woodstock hippie movement and Flower Power made headlines all over the world. The sisters, who have blossomed into modern Malaysian girls with rich cultural exchanges, were still steeped in their Asian values.

At the same time, they appreciated Western liberalization movements and the art of advocating thought leadership.

*We are each our own Masters of the Universe*
*If we do not stand for something, we will fall for anything*
*Love conquers all*

Jade's eldest son did a remarkable job by not
only keeping the company afloat during those
challenging economical times; he then proceeded
to inject funds into the two feisty Phoenix's event.

It took the two Phoenix a total of 2 years to garner
all the support they needed. Finally, the talents,
funds, stage location and government support were
obtained. Their English rose girl friends chipped
in by mailing over ballroom dresses complete with
petticoats, matching leather boots, gloves and
dainty parasols in multiple colors over to Ipoh.

Eventually, their husbands returned from Britain
to act as advisors and helped manage the
production alongside their local comrades.

The location of the event was at the Ipoh Padang (field
in Malay). Set up in 1989, it is in the centre of Ipoh city
against the backdrop of several handsome looking
Colonial buildings. The British used the Padang as a

cricket field in the early 20th century, after which locals used it for football matches and family day events.

It was the year of the Metal Monkey 1980.

According to Chinese horoscope, this metal governed constellation bodes well for those that are success-driven, who pursues their goals with confidence and determination.

Such was the steely determination which drove the two Phoenix to rise above the occasion. What the majority saw as a lost cause, they saw a golden opportunity. An opportunity to remind the founding people of Ipoh that behind every cloud there is always a silver lining. In the midst of despair and hopelessness, the human spirit will triumph.

The Phoenix of Ipoh also knew the importance of creativity and culture. Their close interactions with their friends from all walks of life, nationalities, religion, and creed enlightened their minds.

They remembered a conversation they had
with a European historian cum philosopher
who did missionary work in Ipoh.

"Humans evolved from feeble hunters and gatherers
into sophisticated intellectuals that we are now
through metamorphosis of the mind. Observing,
learning and mimicking from those that have
gone before us. This has been part of human
nature in the past, present and the future."

Jade thought this was so true. She personally saw
how her children grew from babies to toddlers
to adults by mimicking their elder siblings.

*When the student is ready, the teacher appears*
*We are who we surround ourselves with*
*Birds of a feather flock together*

As mothers, both Jade and Teak had inculcated this
ethos during their children's formative years. They

made deliberate attempts to enroll them in public multi-racial schools and organized parties and invited their friends from various cultures and social settings.

*"My child, do not judge your friends by the color of their skin, the language they speak or how much money they have.*
*Look at their heart and character and what have they learned in life.*
*And then you will surely be rich."*

## The LoveStock Parade

The date was set at 16th September, 1980.

The theme was a fusion of art and cultures with love being the core.

Hundreds of people ranging from diplomats, business leaders, academicians, and the general public were expected.

Fireworks, Scottish bagpipes and beating of

gongs opened the parade with great fanfare.

The Malaysian national anthem was sung by

a 12 year old child prodigy from Ipoh.


Jade's eldest son led an 8-man troupe in a

dragon dance performance. This magnificent

30 foot long creature was depicted as chasing a

rare Mother of Pearl, where many have perished

in their quest to obtain this undersea jewel.


Malaysian artisans fronted the parade, and spectators

marveled at the brilliant display of craftsmanship,

fashion, hair art, makeup, music and dance. The two

Phoenix joined in the show by displaying their hand-

sewn qípáo. Jade wore her prized jadeite pins in her

bun, whilst Teak decorated her crowing glory with

Malay jepit rambut or hairpin made out of teak wood.


Talented ladies of Malay, Chinese and Indian

ethnicity proudly paraded their cross-cultural works

of art. From Batik infused qípáo, peonies imprinted sari, henna inspired Baju Kebaya; it was a night of harmonious blend of cultural masterpieces.

The Phoenix's Western sisters ended the night by parading their own version of fusion artwork. Chinese silk tailored evening gowns, matching gloves and colorful parasols which were brought from Britain.

When the song 'Let's do the Twist' was played, dancers popped onto the stage clad in Sakura patterned tweed mini skirts with tank tops and retro themed samfu. This caused an outburst of cheers, whistles and applause from the overly delighted crowd.

To top it all off, a renowned English singer performed a sultry version of Saloma's 'Bila Larut Malam' as a grand finale to a magical night.

## Zhū 珠 Pearl

*Illuminate*

Now 6 months have passed since LoveStock
Parade launched with resounding success.

The event garnered international media attention
and was endorsed by the local Malaysian Tourism
Board to be showcased as a yearly event. LoveStock
reinvigorated the tourism and culture industry in Ipoh,
an area which had been almost dormant since the
demise of the tin mine boom. The Phoenixes saw its
untapped potential and leveraged off what was already
there. They did not have to reinvent the wheel, just

setting it back into motion. Ipoh's natural surroundings, its rich culture and heritage, global friends' goodwill and most importantly the local people's camaraderie was the secret behind LoveStock's success.

The two Phoenix's pictures were featured in several international lifestyle magazines and even appeared on highly acclaimed female talk shows.

This went beyond their wildest dreams.

What began as a simple mission to inject hope and life back into people's lives in their beloved town catapulted them into international stardom.

"Madam Jade, Madam Teak, please tell us how you two ladies managed to pull off this feat?"

"Madam Phoenixes, can you replicate this in London?

In Chicago? In Shanghai? We want
LoveStock everywhere!"


This book was not about finding hidden pearls
in the depths of the ocean. It was also not
about examining and scrutinizing previous
poet's ode to this sacred underwater gem.


This book was a simple tale about Jade 玉 yu
and Teak 柚 you, two Chinese ladies from vastly
different backgrounds, whom, through destiny
see their lives crossing paths and cementing an
enduring sisterly bond spanning a few decades.


How two Daughters of War became Icons of Hope.


It is a story of the often underrated soft power.
A tale about the beauty that lies in every culture.


It is a story about how women can overcome any
obstacles thrown at them; they just need to look within.

It is a reminder of the importance of having good

sisters, blood or association, born or by choice.


Women are bearers of hope, love personified,

nurturers for the weary and lost.


Lovely beings that dazzle and shine

during the darkest hours.


*We are Zhū 珠 Pearls*

*So go*

*Illuminate the world*